FAVORITE MOTHER GOOSE RHYMES

Peter Piper

The Child's World®

Distributed by The Child's World®
1980 Lookout Drive • Mankato, MN 56003-1705
800-599-READ • www.childsworld.com

Acknowledgments
The Child's World®: Mary Berendes, Publishing Director
The Design Lab: Kathleen Petelinsek, Design

Library of Congress Cataloging-in-Publication Data
Beacon, Dawn.
 Peter Piper / illustrated by Dawn Beacon.
    p. cm.
 ISBN 978-1-60954-282-5 (library bound: alk. paper)
 1. Nursery rhymes. 2. Childrens' poetry. [1. Nursery rhymes.] I. Title.
 PZ8.3.B3713Pe 2011
 398.8—dc22
 [E]   2010032417

Printed in the United States of America in Mankato, Minnesota.
December 2010
PA02073

ILLUSTRATED BY DAWN BEACON

Peter Piper picked a peck
of pickled peppers.

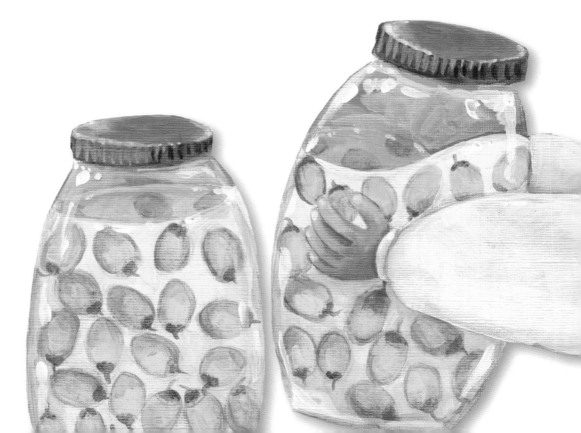

WITHDR...

5

A peck of pickled peppers
Peter Piper picked.

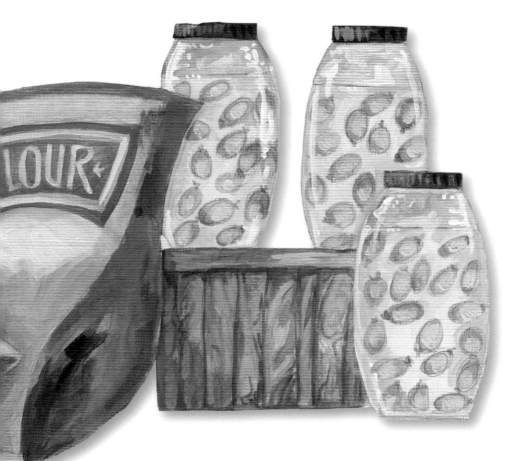

If Peter Piper picked a peck of pickled peppers,

where's the peck of
pickled peppers

Peter Piper picked?

ABOUT MOTHER GOOSE

We all remember the Mother Goose nursery rhymes we learned as children. But who was Mother Goose, anyway? Did she even exist? The answer is . . . we don't know! Many different tales surround this famous name.

Some people think she might be based on Goose-footed Bertha, a kindly old woman in French legend who told stories to children. The inspiration for this legend might have been Queen Bertha of France, who died in 783 and whose son Charlemagne ruled much of Europe. Queen Bertha was called Big-footed Bertha or Queen Goosefoot because one foot was larger than the other.

The name "Mother Goose" first appeared in Charles Perrault's *Les Contes de ma Mère l'Oye* ("Tales of My Mother Goose"), published in France in 1697. This was a collection of fairy tales including "Cinderella" and "Sleeping Beauty"—but these were stories, not poems. The first published Mother Goose nursery rhymes appeared in England in 1781, as *Mother Goose's Melody; or Sonnets for the Cradle*. But some of the verses themselves are hundreds of years old, passed along by word of mouth.

Although we don't really know the origins of Mother Goose or her nursery rhymes, we *do* know that these timeless verses are beloved by children everywhere!

ABOUT THE ILLUSTRATOR

Dawn Beacon lives with her husband and son in the beautiful mountains of Colorado. Her lifelong dream was to be an artist. Since becoming a mom, Dawn finds her greatest inspiration in creating artwork for children. When she is not painting, she loves snowboarding, biking, and hiking with her family.